EROTIC
Advent Calendar

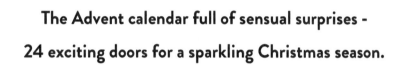

**The Advent calendar full of sensual surprises -
24 exciting doors for a sparkling Christmas season.**

This is how it works: Open the doors together, preferably in the morning or early in the day. You decide whether you want to master every task or see the doors as inspiration for the day.

Some tasks require costumes, sex toys or other accessories. Look at the tasks in advance to prepare yourself, or just let yourself be surprised.

Have fun discovering!

DECEMBER 1

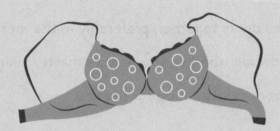

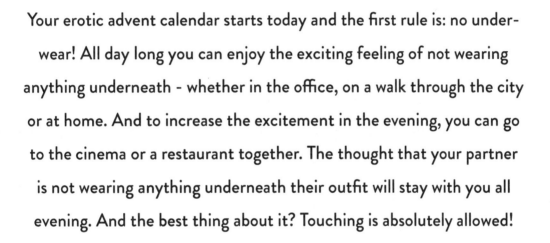

UNDERWEAR PROHIBITED

Your erotic advent calendar starts today and the first rule is: no underwear! All day long you can enjoy the exciting feeling of not wearing anything underneath - whether in the office, on a walk through the city or at home. And to increase the excitement in the evening, you can go to the cinema or a restaurant together. The thought that your partner is not wearing anything underneath their outfit will stay with you all evening. And the best thing about it? Touching is absolutely allowed!

DECEMBER 2

A NEW SEX POSITION

Take some time today to try out new positions together. Choose five new positions that you would like to try out, either individually or together. You can find inspiration on the Internet or in a book about sex positions. How about the „deckchair", the „Indrani" position or the „bridge pillar" for more athletic couples? Show your flexibility and surprise your partner with your skills - and then off to the fun!

DECEMBER 3

STRIP POKER

All you need today is a deck of 52 cards and a few chips. Distribute a small number of chips and play until one of you has lost all of them. The loser has to discard an item of clothing. Then you start the game again. You can find the poker rules online, but you can also play other card games. The most important thing: the stakes remain your clothing!

DECEMBER 4

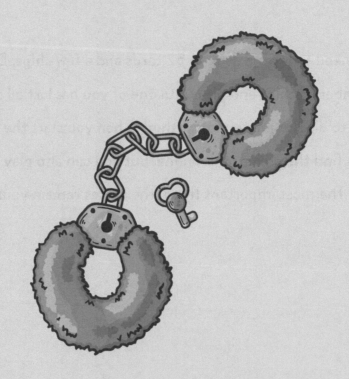

GO HARD

In keeping with the cold season, you show your lustful, cold side today. She takes on the role of the dominatrix, and he must submit to her wishes and demands. Get down to business! The use of handcuffs, a blindfold, a whip or a crop is desirable. Alternatively, a wooden spoon can be used. Tip: Set a „safe word" in case it becomes necessary for harder games.

DECEMBER 5

DIRTY TALKING

Dirty thoughts turn into naughty words and hints. Today is the perfect opportunity to express your thoughts without inhibitions. Share what you think is naughty and what you would like to do with the other person. If you are not alone, whisper in each other's ears and do not hold back. Be surprised where this leads...

DECEMBER 6

NAKED CLEANING

Christmas is approaching and Santa Claus is on his way to bring presents. It's the perfect time to decorate your apartment or house and clean it. To make things even more exciting, take off your clothes! Looking is allowed, but touching is taboo. Santa Claus will only come to you if you behave well. Get excited!

DECEMBER 7

LINGERIE SHOPPING

Treat yourself to a little early Christmas present and buy yourself some new, sexy lingerie from your favorite store. What do you think of classic red for the festive mood or something completely new in bright neon colors? Discuss it together or let the other person decide. Whether you want to try out the new pieces right away and wear them for each other or wait until Christmas to put them under the tree is entirely up to you.

DECEMBER 8

PORN NIGHT

Today we're planning a relaxed movie night. Make yourself comfortable in front of the TV and choose an exciting erotic film that appeals to both of you - both in terms of genre and actors. Let the scenes inspire you and get you in the mood! It's important to watch at least two different sex scenes in full without touching each other. This challenge will only increase the anticipation and desire for each other!

DECEMBER 9

1 _____

2 _____

3 _____

4 _____

5 _____

WRITING A WISH LIST

Today is the perfect opportunity to explore your secret fantasies! Each of you should write down 5 sexual desires on a piece of paper that you haven't tried with your partner yet or that you haven't dared to tell them about. Alternatively, you can write down your 5 favorite sexual activities if there is nothing you haven't done yet. Then put your pieces of paper in a tin or jar for later. Who knows, maybe one day these desires will become reality!

DECEMBER 10

CANDLELIGHT DINNER

Bring romance right into your own four walls! Prepare a delicious meal with starter and dessert while soft music plays in the background and the room is lit only by candlelight. Dress elegantly and let yourself be enchanted by the atmospheric atmosphere. Use this sensual environment to focus your full attention on each other. Whether you want to start the evening relaxed or it gets hot and exciting is entirely up to you. Just go with the flow and enjoy the moment!

DECEMBER 11

HER DAY

Today is all about getting to grips with her body. Explore and discover every inch of her skin. She can sit back and relax while he uses all his skills to give her pleasure. Show her how much you value and adore her. Massaging, stroking, touching, sex - everything is allowed, with or without toys. Let your creativity run wild and enjoy the time together!

DECEMBER 12

SEXTING

Hot messages and saucy pictures: Today sexting is on the agenda - the perfect mix of eroticism and messaging. Write each other sensual messages throughout the day and be as open as possible. What would you like to do together right now? What thoughts are buzzing around in your head? Exchange pictures that make you want more. If necessary, sneak off to the toilet and take some exciting photos for your partner. Let your imagination run wild!

DECEMBER 13

QUICKIE

Choose a „game leader" for today by playing a quick round of rock-pa-per-scissors. The loser is then responsible for seducing the other for a quickie. When and where this happens is entirely up to you and ensures the necessary excitement. Maybe a quick ride on the washing machine? In the shower? Or even out and about in a changing room? Be creative and let yourself be surprised!

DECEMBER 14

NEW LOOK

Breathe new life into your intimate hairstyle! How about a runway, a triangle or a heart-shaped design? Talk to your partner about what they would like. New make-up, a different hair color or a new beard style can also contribute to the change. Do you have creative ideas for each other's look? Be open and dare to try something new!

DECEMBER 15

OUTDOOR ACTION

Today is going to be exciting - get out of your own four walls! Have sex in an exciting place outdoors. Whether in the forest, in the tall grass, on an abandoned construction site, in a changing room, at night in the city, in the snow or on the back seat of your car - let your creativity run wild. Think of a place and then off you go! Remember to wear something that can be quickly taken off and put back on again.

DECEMBER 16

EROTIC MASSAGE

Put on some relaxing music, dim the lights and light a few scented candles. Don't forget the massage oil! Pamper each other with a long, sensual full-body massage. Make sure the room temperature is pleasantly warm so that you feel comfortable even naked. Treat yourself to a well-deserved break from the pre-Christmas stress today.

DECEMBER 17

EROTIC ROLE PLAY

Slip into a different role and let yourself be carried away by the world of a new character. Whether as a teacher and student, pilot and stewardess, policewoman and criminal, nurse and patient, knight and princess or pirate - the possibilities are endless! Rummage through your carnival or carnival box and look for suitable costumes. With the right outfit, make-up and shoes, the whole thing will be even more exciting. Choose the role that appeals to you the most!

DECEMBER 18

CHOCOLATE MASSAGE

The chocolate from your Advent calendar is piling up and you don't know what to do with it? No problem! Today we're planning a sensual chocolate massage. Melt the chocolate or use chocolate sauce, spread towels on the bed or the floor and slowly rub the chocolate into your-self. Massage yourself and paint your bodies creatively. Snacking is expressly allowed!

DECEMBER 19

BED BAN

The bed is off limits today, and the whole bedroom is best. The rule for your little door today is: no bed! Your home has so much more to offer. Look around and discover the sensual possibilities: How about in the kitchen? On the tumble dryer or on the balcony? Go on a discovery tour and try out several places at once. Where do you feel most comfortable?

DECEMBER 20

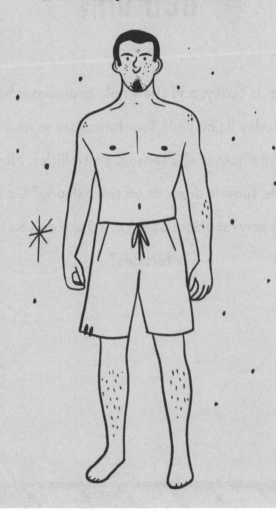

HIS DAY

Today is all about pampering - he can lie down on the bed and relax and she will show him what she can do. Whether it's a seductive strip, tender kisses on his body or a sensual massage - nothing is left out. An intense blowjob, stroking his erogenous zones and a passionate ride to climax ensure that both get their money's worth.

DECEMBER 21

SEXY PHOTO SHOOT

Today is the perfect day to take some hot photos of your partner. Wear his or her favorite outfit, dress up and start a seductive photo session. Slowly let the clothes fall off and show your hottest poses. Make sure there is good light and then make sure you have a safe place where you can save your erotic shots. Capture this exciting moment for eternity.

DECEMBER 22

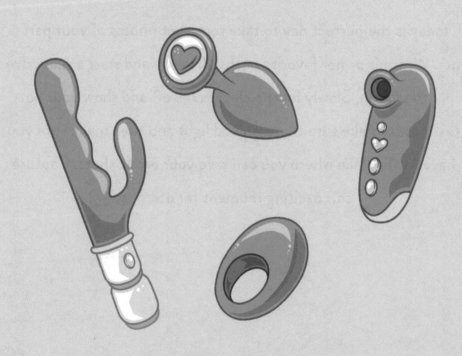

SEX TOYS

The Christmas season is approaching, and today it's all about sex toys! Get out your toy box or go out on the town to treat yourself to something new. Whether it's vibrators, dildos, masturbators, handcuffs, love balls or plugs - anything that gives your lovemaking a new lease of life is in demand today. Let your imagination run wild and discover together what you enjoy the most!

DECEMBER 23

DRAW A WISH

Today is the day your wishes will become reality! Get out the tin, box or jar with your wish lists from day 9 and choose 1, 3 or even all of your wishes. If possible, put them into action immediately. Treat yourself to a glass to relax a little and remember to be considerate of one another. Talk about your wishes, try new things and be inspired by each other's ideas!

DECEMBER 24

XXX-MAS

It's finally Christmas Eve! After enjoying Christmas dinner and exchanging presents, end the evening with a glass of red wine. Now is the perfect time for the second gift giving of the evening. Show your partner the festive, classically elegant lingerie that has been waiting all evening under your clothes for its big appearance. Seduce each other and crown the evening with your shared love!

We hope you had a lot of fun with the

erotic Advent calendar for couples.

Merry Christmas and a great New Year!

Made in United States
Troutdale, OR
12/03/2024

25866551R00031